THE SAND SIFTER

The SÄND SIFTER

Julie Lawson
Illustrated by Anna Mah

Porcépic Press
Victoria

This edition is published by Press Porcépic Limited, 4252 Commerce Circle, Victoria, B.C., V8Z 4M2, with the assistance of the Canada Council.

Canadian Cataloguing in Publication Data

Lawson, Julie, 1947-
   The sand sifter

ISBN 0-88878-288-8

I. Mah, Anna. II. Title.
PS8573.A97S2 1990 jC813'.54 C90-091176-X
PZ7.L39Sa 1990

1

"I've seen the man who makes the sand," Jessica announced as she and Andrew were playing on the beach.

"No you haven't." Andrew kept on shaping the sandy tower of his castle.

"Don't be silly, Jess. He couldn't make all this sand. Just look!" Andrew stretched out his arms to take in the curve of the beach. Sand, sand, sand— to either side of the cove and then beyond to the next one, sand to the tide line, and further out beneath the waves, sand under their feet, deep, deep down as far as you can go. "He just couldn't do it!"

"Well, maybe not all of it. But some. I've seen him."

"No Jess, you haven't." And that put an end

to that. Andrew took his shovel and started digging the moat.

"And he knows all about you, too." Jessica added softly. Too softly for Andrew to hear.

In a tumble-down home carved out of the dunes lived the old man who sifted sand. His home was not a castle of sand, nothing fancy with turrets and towers and winding staircases of periwinkle shells. No gardens of cockles or mussels, no flowery sea anenomes teasing the waters of the moat. No, nothing fancy for the sifter of sand. His home shifted as the weather shifted the sands. In the rainy season it was hard and firm, but on dry days it was like a mist, no more solid than air. On a windy day it curved one way, in a slight breeze it curved another. During a storm it fairly tumbled and toppled on top of him. But it never bothered the old man. Even when it seemed like his home was blowing out from under him and over him and likely to disappear altogether— no, that didn't bother the sifter of sand.

2

It was early in the summer, shortly after moving to Weatherseed that Jessica first heard about the old man.

"He lives in the dunes," her new friend Carey told her. "And he tells stories. You can come with me if you like. I'm going this afternoon."

"O.K! Sure! Can I bring my brother?"

"No, better not this time. And don't tell anybody. Only a few people know about him."

"Will he tell stories if I'm there?" Jessica asked.

"Oh yes! He loves to tell stories. All kinds of stories! He knows everything, and he's been everywhere!"

"He just tells stories?"

"Well … he just tells stories and sifts sand."

"What do you mean, sifts sand?"

"You know... like he takes a handful of sand and puts it in a sieve so that the little bits go through."

"Why would he do that?"

"To make the right sand for our beach, of course."

"Oh," said Jessica. She was not altogether convinced. But she was happy to have a secret.

Later that afternoon Jessica went with Carey to see the sifter of sand. Across the beach they walked, until they came to the dunes. Great masses of sand piled up by the wind, where you could slide and ride as if on the crest of a wave; where you could hide and never be found, or disappear forever, swept up and buried by the shifting sands. Across the dunes they went, climbing up, slipping down, sinking their foot-steps into the sand. Soon they came to the sand sifter's tumble-down home, deep in the dunes. And there they found him.

He was old, old, old. Why, his body was like his home, shifting in the sands. Sometimes he looked so frail and slight you'd think he'd blow away on the wind. But then in the next instant, he'd appear so strong and powerful even the waves could not break him. And his face! Weathered by time, furrowed with lines, like the ridges sculpted in the sand by the tides. It seemed like he'd been there forever, as much a part of the dunes as the wind and the sea.

"Don't shake the sand off before you go inside," Carey said. "He doesn't mind it."

The old man beamed as they entered, and dusted the sand from their feet. Then he swept it into a pile to be sifted.

He was surrounded by pails. Pails of all shapes and shades, colours and sizes. And everywhere you looked were piles of sand! Mountains of sand, peaks and gentle hills of sand! Some pillars stretching up to the ceiling, some no more than a handful. And every pile in its proper place, waiting to be sifted into the proper pail.

And for every type of sand there was a sieve. With big holes, medium, or small. And some so tiny you would hardly know they were there. To sift the fine particles from the coarser ones, and the very fine from the fine, and every type of sand in its proper place.

"My wife's tea strainers," he said with a wink, catching Jessica's eye. "Don't tell her I've got them!"

"I didn't know you had a wife," said Carey.

"I don't," he said with a wink. "But don't tell her that!"

Jessica looked confused. "I don't understand."

"It's just a joke," Carey said. "Don't worry about it." To the old man she explained, "This is Jessica."

"Ah, Jessica! Jessica the wealthy!"

"What?"

"Why, your name! That's what it means!"

"Well, I'm not rich, that's for sure!"

"Oh, but you are! Why, you've just moved into that house up on the cliff, overlooking the cove, haven't you?"

Jessica nodded.

"Well then— you've got the riches of the sea stretching out before you! See, riches come in many forms! Why, you've got the riches of a warm and loving family too, don't you? And not long ago you turned nine years old! And you blew out your birthday candles and wished you didn't have to move to Weatherseed, but your wish didn't come true, did it? 'Cause here you are! And it's better than you thought, isn't it?"

"Oh yes!" Jessica agreed. "Way better!"

"There, you see!" the old man continued. "Sometimes it's better if a wish doesn't come true! And every morning you and your older brother Andrew go for a swim and make sand castles there on the beach. And every afternoon your brother plays in his Boys Only Fort, and you find a few more stones and shells to add to your collection— which you keep in an old cookie tin. And which you keep hidden from that brother of yours!"

"Wow!" Jessica was impressed. "How did you know all that?"

The old man chuckled and gave her a wink. "Why, it's all in the sand! And every grain of sand tells a story. And that's why you've come, isn't it? Not to keep an old man company, no, no, no. But to hear a story!"

"Well, we'll keep you company at the same time, if that's alright!" Jessica said.

"Fine, fine! I'm only teasing, anyway. You can't believe everything you hear, isn't that right, Carey?"

"That's for sure!"

"Except for what the sand sifter tells you.

And that's the honest truth." He settled himself down amongst his pails and piles of sand. Then, taking a sieve in his hand, he began.

He told of far-away places, and long-ago times — when he was young, and the world was young. In hushed tones he spoke of creators and mythical heroes. He spoke of enchanted places, and kingdoms beneath the sea where dragons guarded their treasures, and nymphs floated dreamlike across the sand. And he looked into their eyes as he wove the tales, and held them, entranced. And all the while he spoke, he sifted the sand.

Every grain in its proper place. Into one pail went the pearly grains, into another the misty grays. Into one the bits of sparkling mica; into another, the heavier black-lava grains. And there was a pail for the golden sun-drenched sands, and a pail for the crystally white. Every grain in its proper place, and every grain holding a story.

Day after day Jessica went to see the sand sifter. Sometimes with Carey, sometimes on her own. Her mind danced with the stories he told, and her dreams were filled with the images he created. Often she thought of telling Andrew. But then at the last minute she'd change her mind, and hug the secret to herself.

3

"Hear that ruckus out there?" the old man asked. It was the cry of a raven. "Some believe that's the one that started it all. Life, I mean."

Today the old man was sifting the misty grays, the sand of myths on rugged sea coasts where the raven had created the world.

"Raven. That's the one. He was a spirit, you see, and could change his shape. Why, he could be a baby or an old man or even a spruce needle! But most often he was Raven— sly and cunning, with a gift for mischief! And one day he made the Great Chief of the Sky Kingdom so angry he was sent away for good.

Now below that land of clouds there was nothing but water. Raven flew and flew across the endless sea, looking for a place to land. And what do you suppose that cunning creature did?" asked the old man, sifting, sifting.

"Couldn't he just float on water? Like ducks do?" asked Jessica.

The sand sifter chuckled. "How often do you see ravens on the water?"

"Well, he was a spirit. He could change into a duck."

"Perhaps," said the old man, sifting, sifting. "But that would have been too easy. And the world wouldn't have been created. No, Raven swooped down upon the surface of the sea and beat the water with his wings, beat it with all his anger and frustration until it rose as high as the clouds on either side of him. When the water fell back it did not splash into the sea, nor was it whipped away as spray on the wind. It became land, and there on the first rocky shore Raven was able to rest. And do you know what happened? After a long, long time, those rocks changed to sand. And the sand sifter came along and began to sift the sand, each grain in its proper place. And after a long, long time, trees began to grow. And that land became a cluster of islands."

"Is that how our island got here?" Carey asked.

"There are those who believe it," he smiled.

"But what about the people?"

"Well," began the old man, sifting, sifting, "that poor Raven got lonely. And one day, as he was hobbling along the beach, he reached down and picked up a handful of sand. As the grains slipped through his fingers they made a little pile, almost a little shape. And he looked, and thought, and he looked and thought. Aha! That's what I'll do! So he took another handful and shaped it and shaped it — it was quite wet, you see, so it held the shape pretty well — and soon it became the image of a man. So he did the same thing again, but this time he made a woman. Then he brought them to life. And that was that!"

The old man looked at the tiny grains of sand falling throught the holes of his sieve. "But you know what? We've still got a little of that sand left in us. And that was a good trick of Raven's."

"What do you mean?" asked Carey.

"Well, how much do you remember? From one day to the next or from one year to the next?"

"Not everything, that's for sure!" Jessica said.

"And you haven't even been around long!" the old man laughed. "You see, all things that happen are like grains of sand sifting in our heads.

We've got sieves for brains! Some people have sieves with big holes, and they can't remember a thing. Then there are those who have sieves with small holes. They're the ones who can re-member almost everything. Except for dreams, of course. To remember dreams you've got to have the finest of sieves with the tiniest, tiniest holes. Then you might remember a dream or two."

"What about you? Have you got a sieve for brains?" Jessica asked.

"Why, I'm the sifter of sands," he said with a wink. And that was that.

4

Jessica was pleased with her new expression.

"Sieve for brains, sieve for brains!" she chanted happily to herself. That was what Andrew was, for not believing her. She'd kept the secret for so long, then finally when she was sure the old man wouldn't mind, and even Carey said it was O.K., her stupid brother hadn't even believed her. Well, she'd show him a thing or two.

"Know what, Andrew?" she asked.

"What now, Jessica?" he replied, not looking up from his book.

"You've got a sieve for brains!" she giggled.

Andrew was not amused. He looked at her, frowning. "What did you say?"

"Nothing," she replied, afraid he was angry. She turned to go.

"No, wait a minute! What did you say?"

"I just said you've got a sieve for brains. It was a joke, it's not true!"

"But how did you know?"

"What do you mean?"

"How did you know my dream?"

"What dream?" She was very confused.

"Look, last night I had this dream. And my brain was a sieve— it was just full of holes, great big holes. And there was this black bird flying around and around, dropping stuff into my head, and it all just passed through. So I'm just curious—how did you know about a sieve for brains?"

Jessica found it strange too. Her brother's dream reminded her of the sand sifter's story. And yet Andrew hadn't heard it, and she certainly hadn't told him.

"Did Carey tell you about it?"

"No, I haven't seen her all day."

"Well, you know the old man I told you about? The one that makes sand and tells stories?

"Yeah, but what's that got to do with it?"

"That was in his story, the sieve for brains, and not being able to remember things. And the black bird, that was Raven. In his story."

"When did you hear all this?"

"Yesterday. Remember, this morning I tried to tell you about him. And you didn't believe me," she added. Well, maybe he'd believe her now.

"Are you going to see him again?"

"Yes, I go every afternoon. I love going to see him. He's like a — oh, I don't know — a wizard, sort of. But he doesn't do magic tricks or anything like that."

"He just makes the sand," Andrew said with a slight sneer.

"You can see for yourself, if you come with me. But if you don't want to, I don't care. So there, sieve for brains."

5

Of course Andrew decided to go. He wouldn't let his younger sister get the better of him. And after all, if it turned out to be a laugh, he could get countless days of teasing out of it.

"Ah! This must be Andrew, who remembers his dreams but doesn't always believe his sister! Come in, come in!" The old man greeted them warmly, as always. Today he was sifting the golden-red sand, each grain round and gleaming like a miniature sun. "Tell me," he said, leaning towards them, "did you see any footprints on the beach?"

They looked at each other, and shrugged. "No," Carey said, "not really."

"Tch, tch, tch," said the old man, shaking his head. "You've got to be on the lookout for footprints in the sand! Why, there's no telling where those footprints might lead! And there's no telling what treasures you might find when you follow them!"

"I never thought of that!" Andrew exclaimed. He promised himself he would pay attention to footprints from now on, especially if treasures might be involved.

"Why, once long ago, when I was young and the world was young, I followed some footprints across the sand. Golden-red sand it was, like this," he said, sifting, sifting. "Far and away on the other side of the world it was. Far and away in time," he added softly.

"Were they big footprints?" Jessica asked.

"My, but you are the inquisitive one, aren't you?" the old man chuckled. Andrew and Carey laughed too.

"What's quisitive?" Jessica felt she was being made fun of.

"It's asking a lot of questions," Andrew explained.

"Like in a quiz," added Carey.

"Like curious ... or just plain nosy!" the old man said. They all laughed at that. "But to answer your question, no, the footprints weren't big. Or little. Just medium. Nothing strange about them at all. You know, five toes on each one, the usual sort of thing."

"So the person was barefoot!" noted Andrew the detective.

"Ah yes ... barefoot he was. And why not, seeing as he'd just come from the bottom of the sea! But that part comes later. Now, as I was saying, I followed those footprints across the sandy beach, around one cove, and then another. And soon I came to a young man. He was sitting up on a rock, sad as sad could be, gazing out to sea. And in his hands he held a box." The old man paused, and looked at them intently. "Now then, what do you suppose was in that box?"

"Treasure!" exclaimed Andrew. "Gold coins and jewels!"

"I think there was just one gigantic pearl!" said Carey.

"Well," said Jessica thoughtfully, "I think maybe it was some special shells that he'd been collecting. That's why he was on the beach." It made sense. That's what she would have put in the box.

"So what was it?" Andrew asked.

"Well now, I asked the young man the same question. And he told me a very strange tale.

You see, one day he had come upon a group of boys on the beach. They were all yelling and laughing and waving sticks, and banging down on something, there in the sand. He saw that it was a giant sea turtle, and the poor creature was suffering terribly. So the man scared off those boys, and carried the turtle to the sea. He set him down gently in the water, and watched as the turtle swam away. Well now, he didn't think too much about it until the next day. Then, as he was swimming in the waves, he felt something strange happening."

The old man paused for a moment, as if remembering. He scooped up another sieveful of sand, then continued the sifting and the story. "Something very strange, as though a lightness were passing over him. He couldn't feel the weight of his body anymore, and it seemed as if something were carrying him through the waves. He also noticed that he was getting farther and farther away from shore."

"I know," Jessica said suddenly. "I know! The sea turtle is there and he's riding the turtle!"

"Well, my oh my!" exclaimed the old man. "Who's telling the stories around here! You are absolutely right! The turtle is there, and it's taking the man to the kingdom beneath the sea."

"As a reward?" asked Carey.

"As a reward," replied the old man. "Down, down, down they went, down to the bottom of the sea. And strange as it seems, that man could breathe under the water!"

"And was there treasure in the kingdom?" asked Andrew eagerly.

"Ah, yes! Glittering sea-green emeralds, and sapphires the colour of the sky. And rubies that would tear your heart, so lovely they were. Rubies of a thousand sunsets! Why, every jewel under the sun was there under the sea! But the most beautiful of all were the pearls, gleaming pure and white, shimmering with light." The old man's eyes sparkled at the thought of it. "And what do you suppose that man did?"

"Grabbed a handful and went back to land! That's what I'd do!" said Carey.

"I'd fill up all my pockets first," said Andrew.

"I'd just want to stay there forever and ever!" said Jessica.

"There she goes again! said the old man with a wink. "Why that's what that young man did— well, for a long while anyway. He stayed in the kingdom beneath the sea. And he fell in love

with the Sea King's daughter and he stayed there, surrounded by riches and happy as a clam."

"Happy as a clam!" Andrew laughed. "I bet they were happy clams, with all their pearls!"

"No silly," said Jessica. "It's oysters that have pearls, not clams. Even I know that."

"But you know," continued the old man, "even though he had the love of his princess and all the jewels he could ever imagine, he was missing something. It started as a kind of tug, a gentle tug, but then it got stronger and more forceful until he could ignore it no longer. And that force was the land, pulling him back. He had to get back to the land. Now his princess told him that once he left the kingdom under the sea he could never return. Still, he insisted. So his broken-hearted princess called the turtle to take him home. But before he left she gave him a little box. And she said, "Take this to remember me, but don't ever open the box.""

"How could he stand it?" Andrew wondered. "Wasn't he the least bit ... inquisitive?"

"Well yes, he was. And it was a painful decision for him to make. But he promised, and the turtle came, and off they went back to the land.

And when he got back, why, he noticed that everything had changed! The beach had changed,

his village had changed, the forest had changed—
why the forest was gone completely! Now there
were fields and houses where there used to be
trees. And he walked to the village, looking for
his house. And he couldn't find it anywhere. And
the people all had changed! He couldn't believe
it! He had only been gone a short time! And after
awhile he came across an old fellow that had a
familiar look about him, and he described his
parents, and his old home, and asked could he
explain what had happened. And now that old
man looked at him in fright, as if he had seen a
ghost. And he said, why all that's been gone for
300 years!"

"300 years!" exclaimed Jessica. "What a
shock!"

"That's one way of putting it!" the old man
said.

"So what did he do?" asked Carey.

"Well, he was greatly perplexed, as you can
imagine. So he took his little box and he walked
across the sandy beach and came to a big rock.
And there he sat, wondering what to do."

"And that's where you found him, right?" asked
Jessica.

"Yes indeed. And he told me his troubles—
how he could never go back to his princess, but

could never live here, since everything and everyone he'd love on the land was gone." Thoughtfully the old man sifted his sand. "And so I said to him, why don't you open the box? Maybe that will help you decide."

"But he promised!" Jessica was outraged.

"Yes, he'd promised, but he was in a such a sad state he opened the box. And there was nothing in the box but SAND!" The old man paused dramatically. "And he poured out the sand, just like this!"

The old man took a handful of golden-red sand and they watched, entranced, as the tiny grains trickled through his fingers. "And as the grains of sand fell to the ground, why time itself just fell from that young man's face. And before my very eyes his youth disappeared forever! The sands of time changed him to an old, old man. And he got his wish and returned to the land alright, but not in the way he'd wanted."

The children watched the sand trickling through the old man's fingers, then stared at his face, afraid the same thing might happen— there before their eyes.

But the old man caught their look, and laughed. "Don't you worry! Nothing like that's going to happen to me! I'm the sifter of sands, remember?" Then he gave them a wink, and shooed them gently out the door.

"What did you think? I was right, wasn't I?" Jessica asked as they were walking home.

"Well, I still don't believe he makes the sand. But he tells good stories," Andrew said. He wouldn't admit his sister was right, not in a thousand years.

"In that story, did he mean the man died?" asked Jessica.

"Of course!" Andrew said. "Don't you understand anything? What do you think would happen to someone who instantly turned 300 years old?"

"So ... if he hadn't opened the box, he would have stayed young forever?"

"Right! That's what you get when you rescue a sea turtle. So keep your eyes open, Jess!"

And she did, all the way home across the sandy beach. But she didn't see a single one. Nor any footprints, either. And even though she didn't exactly understand the word, she thought she was feeling perplexed.

6

Andrew didn't mean to spoil things. It just kind of slipped out. After all, he hadn't promised Jessica he wouldn't tell anybody. And Carey had said there were a few other people who knew, so it wasn't as if he were giving a big secret away. And in all the times they'd been to the dunes, never once had the old man told them not to tell. So.

It happened in the Boys Only Fort, when he and a couple of friends were talking about dreams.

"I never have dreams," said Rob. "Or if I have them, I never remember when I wake up."

"I usually remember mine," said Nathan. "The other night I had this really cool dream. There was this whale riding on two dragons and it got really angry and changed into this gigantic bird, and its wings were so huge the whole sky turned black. And the wings were getting closer and closer, and beating in my face, and finally I woke up!"

"And the wings made thunder, right?" asked Andrew.

"Yeah! Hey, how did you know?"

"'Cause that's one of the old man's stories."

"What old man?" asked Rob.

Well, Andrew had put his foot in his mouth alright, and it was too late to back out now. He might as well make the most of it. "The old man who sifts sand and tells stories, out on the dunes. Haven't you heard about him?"

"No!" the boys exclaimed. "Tell us!"

Andrew felt quite pleased, seeing as how he knew something they didn't. Especially being a newcomer and all.

"What! You've lived here all your lives and never seen the sand sifter? That's amazing!" And he told them about the old man who sifted the sand, with every pile in its proper place, and every grain holding a story.

"Can we go out there with you?" asked Nathan.

"Sure! I go almost every afternoon, usually with Jess and Carey. Meet me on the beach after lunch, and we'll go!"

"Will he mind?" wondered Rob.

"No," Andrew assured them. Anyway, it was too late now if he did.

After they'd gone, he realized he probably should have told them to keep it a secret. But it was too late now, and that was that.

Now the old man was surrounded by children, as well as his pails and piles of sand. First there had been Carey and Jessica, then Andrew, then Andrew's friends, then all of their friends. For nobody was keeping it a secret anymore.

Every afternoon they met at the cabin in the dunes. Waited quietly while he brushed the sand from their feet and swept it into a pile to be sifted. Then, taking his sieve, he would begin. Sifting, sifting, every grain holding a story, woven into words by the sand sifter.

He spoke of man-eating giants that stalked the woods, and ice witches who dwelt in caverns of snow. He thrilled them with tales of hideous ogres and monstrous demons, of scaly sea serpents and gruesome goblins.

And they shivered with fear and delight, and

kept coming back for more.

"Why do we always go in the afternoon?" Andrew wondered one day. He had buried Jessica in the sand, and except for her head sticking up she looked very much like a miniature dune. Now Andrew was idly letting grains of sand trickle through his fingers, building up hills over her toes.

"I don't know."

"Well, that's what I mean. There's no reason. Let's go at night for a change."

"We're not allowed to go out at night."

"I know, but look— we'll pretend to go to bed, and then sneak out. I've done it before."

"Really?" Jess sat right up, shaking the mountain of sand away. What was even more amazing than Andrew sneaking out at night was that he was telling her about it. "Do you really?"

"Sure. I go out to the fort sometimes, or down to the beach."

"Wow!" sighed Jessica, impressed.

"So that's what we can do. You just sneak into my room, then we climb out the window. It's not that high up. I'll bring a flashlight."

"O.K.!" beamed Jessica. "And you don't have to worry, Andrew, I won't tell, ever."

"I know that. You're dead if you do, right?"

"Right!"

And that was that.

7

In the dunes, Andrew shone his flashlight around until it lit up the outline of the sand sifter's home. Then he switched the light off. It was very dark. Except for the stars and a sliver of a moon there was no light at all. And from the sand sifter's home not even the flicker of a candle.

"Funny there isn't any light in there," said Andrew.

"Maybe he's asleep," whispered Jessica. "We better not wake him up."

"He can't be asleep yet, it's not that late. C'mon, we'll go and see."

Silently they slipped across the sand to his home. The door was open, as always.

"Hello!" Andrew called softly.

No answer.

"Let's go in," he said.

Silently they slipped inside.

Not a sign of him anywhere, except for his pails and piles of sand.

"I think a couple of his pails are gone," said Andrew. "I know he had a shiny one, and it's gone."

"He's probably out collecting sand somewhere," said Jessica.

"Not in the dark!"

Andrew shone his flashlight around the room. "It's strange, isn't it?"

"What?" asked Jessica.

"Well, you never see him anywhere in the village, or on the beach. And nobody else has seen him. Never anywhere except here."

"So? Maybe he likes to keep to himself." Especially now that there's always a crowd, she added to herself. "Andrew, I think we better go. I don't like being here when he's out."

The mountains of sand glittered eerily when caught by the flashlight's beam. They appeared huge and watchful, like sentinels guarding the old man's home. The sands of time, guarding the past. Jessica shivered. "C'mon, Andrew." She walked outside. There were no footprints in the sand, except for their own.

"And you know what else?" Andrew asked as they were walking home. "You never see him eating or drinking. There's never a sign of any food. Or any water. Have you ever noticed that?"

"No, not really," Jessica admitted.

"So what does he eat?" Andrew wondered. "He's got to eat."

"I don't know. Sandwiches?" Jessica laughed.

"Very funny, Jess."

"I know!" she giggled happily. It had been a great adventure, sneaking out to the dunes at night. And she had made a good joke. She didn't care what the sand sifter ate, as long as he kept telling stories.

Every night it was the same. His home silent and still and empty, except for the sentinels of sand. And not a sign of the old man.

But every afternoon, there he'd be, sifting sand and telling stories. And the pails that had been missing in the night would be there the next day, in their proper place, as always. And always the piles of sand, sometimes larger, sometimes smaller.

"He'll never ever sift it all," said Andrew. "Doesn't he ever get tired? Doesn't he ever sleep?"

"I don't know," said Jessica.

"It's funny, isn't it? How nobody ever asks him questions. Just ordinary questions, I mean. We don't really know anything about him."

"No, we don't." Jessica agreed. "And it doesn't even matter, does it?"

8

After a while it seemed that every child in the village was there, and the sand sifter's tumbledown home was fairly bulging. And the ones that couldn't fit inside sat and listened outside, while the old man told the stories and sifted the sand.

"Maybe he doesn't mind," Jessica thought. "He never says. He never tells anybody to go away. So maybe he doesn't mind."

It wasn't the same anymore. Carey didn't care. Andrew didn't care. But Jessica was sorry. Even though he hadn't changed. One person or twenty or fifty— why, it wouldn't bother the sifter of the sand. He had his job to do, and that was that. Still, he always gave a wink to Jessica, as if he were telling the story specially for her. That's how she felt about it, anyway. And besides, once he started spinning his tale, why, it didn't matter at all who was there! Why, the crowd was just as hushed as could be, and all you could hear was the old man's voice and the sand, sifting, sifting. She was woven into the magic and transported— it was as simple as that!

Today he was sifting pale-blue grains of quartz, and as they filtered through the sieve the light caught them and they shone, lustrous and translucent. And he told of how the sun came to be, and the moon, and all the stars. He told of dragons that breathed clouds and made rain, and of enormous eagles that lifted their wings in anger, causing lightning to streak across the sky.

And he spoke of the sand. "Now all these grains of sand hold a story," he said. "And do you think you could ever tell them all? And do you think you could ever count them all?"

"No!" exclaimed the children.

"No indeed— and only a fool would ever try! Why, grains of sand are like the thoughts and dreams of all the people on earth. You could never, ever, know them all!"

"But you do, don't you?" said Jessica.

"Why of course!" he said with a wink. "I'm the sifter of sands!"

9

The summer ambled on and soon it was autumn, a time for endings. And when a mist rolled in from the sea chilling the dunes, Jessica was afraid the stories would end. They didn't. But something different happened.

"See this?" The old man had finished his story, and held up a stone that had somehow got mixed up with the grains of sand. It was the colour of honey, warm as a golden afternoon. And around its centre was a ring of blue. "This is a wishing stone. You can tell a wishing stone because it has a ring around it. Now, the ring doesn't have to be right in the centre like this one. But it does have to be unbroken. It can be any old stone— it doesn't have to be an agate, like this one." He held it so the light could shine through. "Of course, if it is an agate, then you've got a better chance of your wish coming true.

Now suppose I stop sifting for a time and make a wish on this stone! Why, I could wish for all this sand to turn into gold! Or I could wish for it all to disappear! Or I could wish for something else, something unexpected." He looked and looked at the eager faces, at all those children waiting and wondering. And the intensity of that look made them shiver.

Then he spoke, and his words made their hearts stand still. "Why, I wish you would all turn into grains of sand, so I could sweep you into a pile for sifting!"

Well, it seemed for an instant that the sands of time had stopped running altogether, so frozen in fright did all those children feel. And they all just stared at the old man, or at that wishing-stone, terrified to look at each other in case they saw a pile of sand! And it was so, so silent you could almost hear the stories in those grains of sand just bursting to get out!

Then the old man winked, and chuckled. "Come now— what's the matter with you? You don't believe everything you hear, do you?"

They laughed nervously, still a bit uneasy.

"Of course," continued the old man, "everything I told you about the wishing stone is true. It just doesn't work all the time. Sort of has an off-day, you might say. Now... I could try again tomorrow! But you needn't worry. I've got plenty of sand for sifting, and that's the honest truth."

He put the stone in his pocket, and picked up the sieve again. Pearly-gray and misty blue, the grains of autumn streamed their way into the pail. And as the children slipped away he sat there, sifting, sifting.

Jessica was the last to leave, as always. "Goodbye," she said. "And thank you for the stories."

"Here!" He held out the agate. "Take this, Jessica the wealthy."

"Oh!" It gleamed in the palm of her hand, smooth and shimmery as still water. She had never seen anything so beautiful. "Thank you! Oh, thank you!"

"Now you be careful, Jessica! Be careful what you wish for, 'cause your wish may come true!"

Then he winked at her, and went back to his sifting.

10

That night there was a terrific wind that came whistling and wailing from across the sea. Jessica lay awake, worrying about the old man. As soon as it was light she got up and raced along the beach to the dunes.

But his tumble-down home was gone. Now there was nothing but the dunes. Afraid that he had been buried, Jessica frantically began to dig. But she found nothing. Not a trace.

"Maybe it's the wrong place," she thought. "I must have got it wrong." So she began searching— the next dune, and the next, and the next. But she found nothing. No footprints, nothing. Not a trace.

Then suddenly she saw him. High on a ridge, striding along with his pails and sieves hanging from a knapsack on his back.

"Wait!" she called, stumbling up the dune after him. "Wait! Please!"

He reached out a hand and helped her to the top of the ridge.

"Are you going to build a new home?" she asked. "I'll help you!"

"Thank you, Jessica! But no, I'm not building a new home. I'm moving on."

"But why? Why couldn't you just build another home and stay?"

'Well, I could. But I won't. It's the time, you see. The sands are shifting and it's time to move on."

Then Jessica remembered the stone gleaming darkly in her pocket. "Will it come true if I wish for you to stay?" she asked, holding it out to him.

"Ah, Jessica ... there are some things too big for wishes."

"Then I wish you'll come back!"

He put one hand over hers, gently enfolding the stone.

'I will come back, in one way or another," he said. "And I'll leave a dream or two for you to remember."

Jessica felt tears prickling her eyes, and brushed them away. "But ... but I don't even know your name!"

"Just remember me as the Sand Sifter," he said with a wink. Then he patted her on the head and, with a wave of his hand, was gone.

Some time later, Andrew found Jessica crying on the beach.

"What's the matter, Jess?" he asked.

"Nothing."

"Where have you been?"

"Nowhere."

"How come you've got sand in your hair?"

"Never mind." She would tell him, probably. Sometime maybe, but not now. Now she hugged the secret to herself.

"You're going to get it."

"I don't care!" And she didn't, either. For the sand in her hair was the sparkly kind, meant for the finest of sieves. And it came from the sifter of sands, the teller of tales, the maker of dreams.

Where had the old man come from? No one knows.

Where did he go? No one knows.

And no one in Jessica's village ever saw him again.

But somewhere far and away or close in time he sifts his sand and tells his tales.

You won't find him if you go looking.

But you might come upon him by chance one day, as he shifts in and out of the shadowy land of myths and dreams ... sifting, sifting.

And if you do, stay for a moment and listen!

Author's Notes

Myths

The art of story-telling is older than written literature, older than recorded history. Through myths, the story-teller expressed what early man knew about his world and what he believed to be true.

Since story-telling was— and is—an oral tradition, many tales are changed in the telling. Each story-teller enlivens and enriches the story in his own way— adding here, interpreting there. The result is a tremendous richness of stories, often with the same theme but with many variations.

So it is with the sand sifter, whose stories were taken from early sources but adapted to fit his tales. His re-telling of the creation myth is adapted from "The Beginning of the Haida World", found in *Indian Legends of Canada* by Ella Elizabeth Clark (Toronto: McClelland & Stewart, 1960). Raven the Trickster-Creator is the central figure in many West Coast Indian myths, with different versions explaining how he created the world and mankind. The sand sifter's version is yet another.

The sand sifter's second story is an old Japanese tale containing elements common to many myths: magic, for instance, and the "goodness is rewarded" theme. Certain aspects of the story also bear a resemblance to the "Rip van Winkle" tale.

There are many versions of this story, the oldest going back to the 8th Century. The events are said to have actually happened in the year 477 to a fisherman named Urashima. The version told by the sand sifter is adapted from "The Young Urashima" which appears in *Japanese Tales and Legends*, retold by Helen and William McAlpine (London: Oxford University Press, 1958).

A Word About Sand

Sand is made from rocks, worn down over millions of years by water and wind. Grains of sand really do come in different sizes, shapes and colours, with dull bits and sparkly bits— although perhaps the sand sifter has a few varieties known to him alone!

But there are golden-white dunes at Long Beach, British Columbia, waiting to be climbed. On the Hawaiian Island of Maui there are black sand beaches, while on neighboring Kauai, round pearly grains of beige and orange trickle through fingers. Yellow sand drifts down from the Gobi Desert in Northern China, and on the beaches of Canada's West Coast, wet gray sand is perfect for building castles.